Mr. Tanen's Ties Rule!

by
Maryann
Cocca-Leffler

Albert Whitman & Company
Morton Grove, Illinois

To the students at Spring Valley Elementary School, Spring Valley, CA. Thank you.

Maryann Cocca-Leffler

Note! Career Day — Tuesday

To Olivia Spofford— You're a Star! ♡ Auntie!

Also by Maryann Cocca-Leffler

Bravery Soup • *Jungle Halloween* • *Missing: One Stuffed Rabbit*
Mr. Tanen's Ties • *Mr. Tanen's Tie Trouble*

Library of Congress Cataloging-in-Publication Data

Cocca-Leffler, Maryann, 1958-
Mr. Tanen's ties rule! / written and illustrated by Maryann Cocca-Leffler.
p. cm.
Summary: On Career Day, Principal Tanen distributes "Job" ties to the students who will run Lynnhurst School for
the day while he and the teachers become students, but important surprise visitors arrive in the midst of the ensuing chaos.
ISBN 0-8075-5308-5 (hardcover)
[1. Schools—Fiction. 2. School principals—Fiction. 3. Neckties—Fiction. 4. Occupations—Fiction.] I. Title: Mister Tanen's ties rule!. II. Title.
PZ7.C638Mrr 2005 [E]—dc22 2004018579

The design is by Maryann Cocca-Leffler.

For more information about Albert Whitman & Company, please visit our web site at www.albertwhitman.com.

Please visit www.maryanncoccaleffler.com.

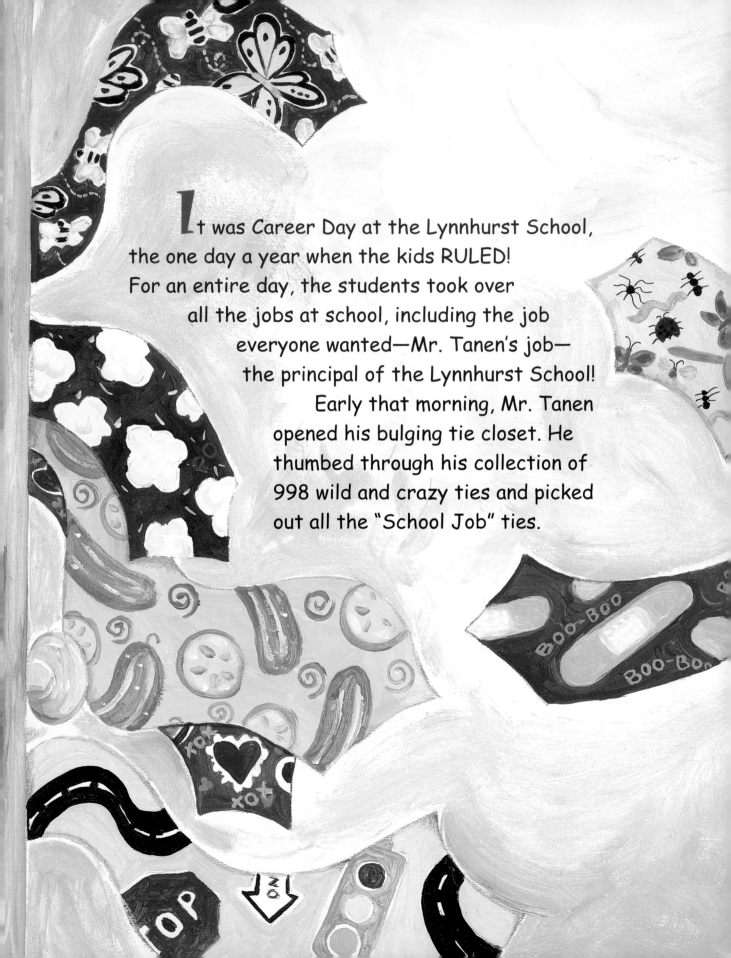

It was Career Day at the Lynnhurst School, the one day a year when the kids RULED! For an entire day, the students took over all the jobs at school, including the job everyone wanted—Mr. Tanen's job— the principal of the Lynnhurst School!

Early that morning, Mr. Tanen opened his bulging tie closet. He thumbed through his collection of 998 wild and crazy ties and picked out all the "School Job" ties.

Mr. Tanen was known throughout the school and the town for his tie collection. His arms filled with ties, he headed to the auditorium where the kids were anxiously waiting.

Career Day always started with the "Tie Ceremony." One by one, Mr. Tanen picked the lucky students' names from a big box. Each student came on stage and was given a Job Tie. This year, Kristin would be the art teacher, Alex the music director, Maria the science teacher, and Leo the cook.

Mr. Tanen handed out all the ties—

except
one.

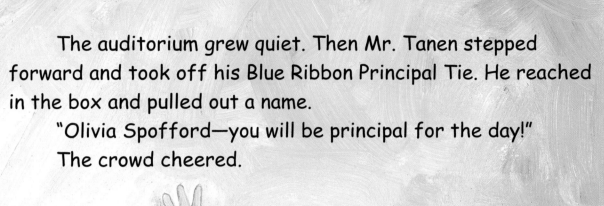

The auditorium grew quiet. Then Mr. Tanen stepped forward and took off his Blue Ribbon Principal Tie. He reached in the box and pulled out a name.

"Olivia Spofford—you will be principal for the day!"

The crowd cheered.

The kids lined up, wearing their ties and ready to RULE. A tieless Mr. Tanen explained, "Today you will do the jobs we do every day, and we will take your place as students. Principal Olivia, you are in charge. Here are the keys to my office AND my tie closet."

Olivia stretched on tiptoe to reach the microphone.

"Okay, school. I am Miss Olivia, your new principal. We are going to have recess now."

Mr. Tanen whispered to Olivia, "It's only 8:30 in the morning!"

Then he smiled. "It's official," he thought. "The kids have taken over the school!"

Back at the School Department, the director, Mr. Apple, was meeting with Mrs. Harding. She was from the Education Department in Washington, D.C.

"Mrs. Harding, we are so proud that the Lynnhurst School has been nominated for the National School Award," said Mr. Apple as he nervously handed her a folder. "As you will see, this school is one of the finest in the nation."

"Mr. Apple, *on paper* it looks like a fine school," said Mrs. Harding as she flipped through the folder. "But before giving out the award, I must see every school for myself. The Lynnhurst School is the last school I need to visit."

"Of course," said Mr. Apple. "Let's go there right now. You'll be very impressed."

As Mr. Apple and Mrs. Harding entered the school, they came upon kids washing the windows in the front hall. Sammy was giving the orders.

Mrs. Harding wrote something in her notebook. Mr. Apple was puzzled. "Where is Ms. Jan, the janitor?" he thought.

When they reached the principal's office, a small head poked up from behind the desk.

"May I help you?" asked Colleen.

"Uhhh, yes, we are here to see the principal," said Mr. Apple.

Colleen dialed the phone. "Hello, Principal? Mr. Apple and a lady are here to see you."

Then Colleen looked at Mr. Apple. "The principal wants to know what this is about."

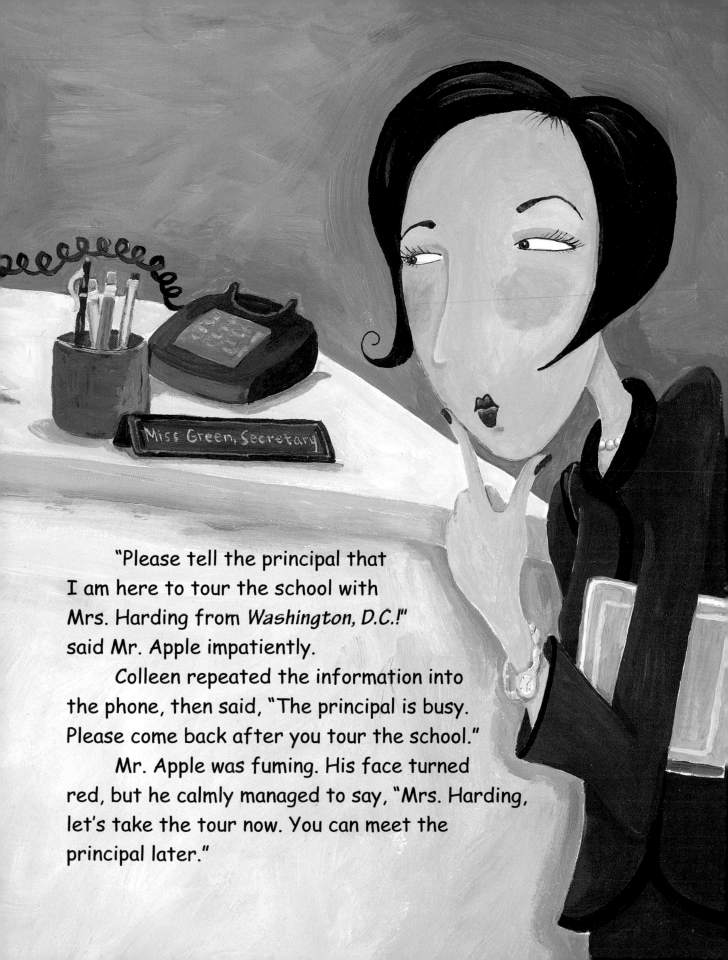

"Please tell the principal that I am here to tour the school with Mrs. Harding from *Washington, D.C.!*" said Mr. Apple impatiently.

Colleen repeated the information into the phone, then said, "The principal is busy. Please come back after you tour the school."

Mr. Apple was fuming. His face turned red, but he calmly managed to say, "Mrs. Harding, let's take the tour now. You can meet the principal later."

Meanwhile, Mr. Tanen was spending his day as a student. He knew all the spelling words,

volunteered to help in math class,

and sang his heart out
in music.

Mr. Apple and Mrs. Harding made their way around the school. Kristin's art class was painting a giant mural,

and Maria led the science class
on a bug-finding expedition.

Maria proudly showed Mr. Apple a huge beetle.
Mrs. Harding silently scribbled in her notebook.
"This tour is not going well!"
thought Mr. Apple.

In the cafeteria, Leo's creation—
the super-duper-tuna-and-peanut-butter
taco—was a big hit.

In history class, Mrs. Harding got all wrapped up in the Ancient Egypt lesson. Then she wrote furiously in her notebook.

"Oh, no!" Mr. Apple said to himself. "This is a disaster!"

As they passed the gym, Mr. Apple noticed a rather large student. He rubbed his eyes.

"It can't be!" he thought. "I must be seeing things!"

Finally, Mr. Apple and Mrs. Harding returned to the principal's office. This time Mr. Apple was firm.

"Now, Colleen, I really need to see Mr. Tanen."

"But Mr. Apple," said Colleen, "You never said you wanted to see *Mr. Tanen*. You said you wanted to see the *principal*. Olivia is our principal today."

The door to Mr. Tanen's office opened.

"I am the principal, Miss Olivia!" said Olivia.
"Welcome, Mrs. Harding!"

Mr. Apple lost his temper. "What's going on in this school?" he shouted. "Where is Mr. Tanen?"

"Oh, Mr. Tanen is in gym class, probably playing kickball," said Olivia.

"Playing kickball?" repeated Mrs. Harding.

"I would be happy to get him," said Colleen.

"But first you would need to write a note to dismiss him from class."

Mr. Apple rolled his eyes and quickly wrote the note. Colleen ran off toward the gym.

Mr. Apple looked at Mrs. Harding. She was writing in her notebook again.

"RATS! The Lynnhurst School will never get the award now," Mr. Apple thought.

Within minutes, Mr. Tanen ran panting into the office. "Yes, Miss Olivia? You wanted to see me?"
Mr. Apple did not look happy.
"Mr. Tanen, these fine people would like to speak with you," said Olivia. "You may use my office."

The meeting went on for an hour. Mr. Tanen told Mrs. Harding all about Career Day and, of course, about his tie collection. When they came out of the office, Mr. Apple and Mrs. Harding were smiling and wearing ties.

"Mr. Tanen," said Mrs. Harding. "I have never seen a school where the students were so excited about learning. You have truly made learning FUN." She opened her bag and pulled out a certificate.

"I hereby declare Lynnhurst School the winner of the National School Award!"

The students all cheered.

Mrs. Harding continued, "Mr. Tanen, you and your students will be invited to Washington, D.C.!"

Olivia draped the Washington, D.C., tie around Mr. Tanen's neck.

"Mr. Tanen," she said, "Here's the perfect tie for the trip!"